And take *Mulan* for only $3.99*!

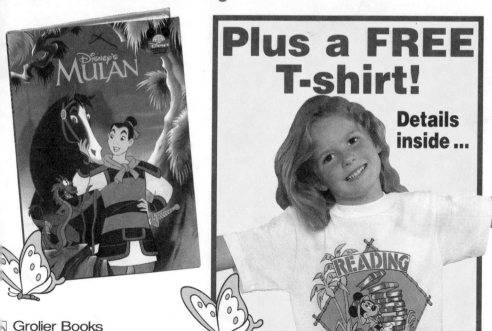

Plus a FREE T-shirt!

Details inside ...

P9-CSG-083

Disney stories are so alive your child feels part of them!

Simba. 101 Dalmatians. Winnie the Pooh. Cinderella. Dumbo and more! Disney magic makes these characters so real they become friends forever. And that friendship can lead to a lifelong love of reading. Now you and your child can share the wonder and delight of all your own favorite childhood friends in *DISNEY'S WONDERFUL WORLD OF READING.* It's a collection that guides your child along the road of imagination to the fun and excitement of reading.

Start your exploration of the world of reading with this marvelous FREE BOOK OFFER. See the attached cards for all the details — then return one today to introduce your child to all the magic of *DISNEY'S WONDERFUL WORLD OF READING!*

Begin with **7 books FREE** and one more for **$3.99***
when you agree to take only 4 more shipments of 2 books each!

Plus a FREE Mickey Mouse T-Shirt!

Say "Yes!" to this special offer!

Attention Parents:

Since 1973, millions of children and their families have enjoyed membership in DISNEY'S WONDERFUL WORLD OF READING®. We're sure you and your child will, too. So sure, in fact, we're not asking you to risk even a penny.

We'll send your child 7 classic Disney Storybooks FREE and one more for only $3.99*. Plus a FREE Mickey Mouse T-shirt!

Once you've shared these wonderful books with your little one, we're certain you'll both want more.

But it's up to you. It costs you nothing to try the trial book for 10 days. We even pay the return postage if you decide not to keep it. No matter what you decide, the 7 FREE books and FREE Mickey Mouse T-shirt are yours as our gift, <u>no strings attached</u>!

See for yourself. Detach one of the cards now, while it's on your mind. Take it home, fill it out and mail your child's Free Gift Certificate today.

Sincerely,

Dan Cirilli

Dan Cirilli
President
Grolier Books

Note: if cards are missing, write to:

Disney's Wonderful World of Reading
P.O. Box 1771
Danbury, CT 06816-1771

Published by Grolier Books
© 1996 Disney Enterprises, Inc.
No portion of this book may be
reproduced without the written
consent of Disney Enterprises, Inc.
Produced by Bumpy Slide Books
Printed in the United States of America
ISBN: 0-7172-8756-4

GROLIER
BOOK CLUB EDITION

Walt Disney's
Winnie the Pooh and Tigger Too

It was a sunny morning in the Hundred-Acre Wood. Pooh was spending it in his Thoughtful Spot trying to concentrate.

"Think! Think! Think!" he said to himself. But Pooh's thinking was soon interrupted.

Pooh was suddenly bounced to the ground. "Hello, I'm Tigger!" Tigger exclaimed. "T-I-double grr. That spells Tigger."

"I know," replied Pooh. "You've bounced me before."

"That's right. You're the one who's stuffed with fluff!" Tigger remembered. "Well, I've got to go now. I've got a lot of bouncin' to do!" And before Pooh knew it, Tigger was gone.

Tigger bounced . . . and bounced . . . and bounced . . . until he bounced right into Piglet.

"Tigger, you sc-sc-sc-scared me!" Piglet stammered.

"I did?" wondered Tigger. "Why, that was just one of my little bounces!"

"Oh then, thank you, Tigger," said Piglet.

"Yup! I'm saving my best bounce for old Long Ears!" Tigger announced. And off he bounced to see Rabbit.

Rabbit was enjoying a quiet morning in his garden when Tigger appeared. He bounced right on top of Rabbit, sending vegetables flying everywhere.

Rabbit was very upset. "Why don't you
ever stop bouncing?" he asked Tigger.

"'Cause that's what tiggers do best!"
Tigger said happily.

Then Tigger sang a little song. It explained
how tiggers are bouncy because they are made
out of rubber and springs.

Tigger bounced all over Rabbit's garden as
he sang, happy to be the only tigger in the
whole world. Then off he bounced, leaving
Rabbit's garden in a mess.

Later that day, Rabbit told Pooh and Piglet about his plan to unbounce Tigger.

"We'll take him on a long Explore into the woods," explained Rabbit. "Then we'll lose him there. When we go back for him the next morning, he'll be a sad and sorry Tigger! It will take the bounce right out of him!"

"That is a splendid idea," said Piglet.
But Pooh just snored. He was fast
asleep in a soft chair.

Piglet woke
Pooh up. Then
they all agreed to
take Tigger on an
Explore the very
next day.

It was a cold and misty morning as Pooh,
Piglet, Rabbit, and Tigger set off into the
woods. Tigger bounced on ahead of the others.

Finally, Rabbit decided it was time to lose
Tigger altogether.

Rabbit quickly led the others to a hollow log and told them to hide inside.

Tigger soon came bouncing back.

"Hello-ooo!" he called, wondering where his friends had gone.

Tigger bounced up on top of the log where
Rabbit and Pooh and Piglet were hiding.

"Hello-ooo!" he cried again. No one answered.

"That's funny. They must be lost," Tigger said.
So he bounced away to
find them.

As soon as Tigger was out of sight, Rabbit began leading the way home.

As they walked, it seemed to Pooh and Piglet that they kept passing the same sand pit. But Rabbit insisted they were not lost.

A while later, they arrived at the sand pit again. "We keep looking for home, but we keep finding this pit. Maybe if we looked for this pit, we might find home," Pooh suggested.

"That makes no sense," said Rabbit. "We're not lost. Wait here. I'll prove it to you."

So Pooh and Piglet waited . . .

and waited . . .

and waited.

Pooh's tummy rumbled. At last he said, "Come, Piglet. My honey pots at home are calling to my tummy. I couldn't hear them before because Rabbit was talking."

Sure enough, Pooh's tummy led them home—where Tigger bounced right into them!

Tigger asked Pooh where Rabbit was.
"Missing in the mist," Pooh answered.
"Then I'll just have to bounce him out
of there!" cried Tigger.

Meanwhile, Rabbit was lost and afraid.
He heard unfamiliar noises all around him.
His imagination began to run wild.

CHOMP

The noises seemed to get louder,
but Rabbit wasn't about to wait and
find out what they were.

He ran for safety—and ran straight into
Tigger.

"Tigger!" said Rabbit. "You're not lost!"

"Tiggers never get lost. Let's go home!"
Tigger told Rabbit.

Poor Rabbit. His plan to unbounce Tigger
had not worked out very well. Tigger was still
as bouncy as ever.

The next morning, a blanket of snow
covered the Hundred-Acre Wood. Roo waited
anxiously for Tigger. The little kangaroo loved
spending time with his bouncy friend.

"Can Tiggers climb trees?" Roo asked as
they bounded through the snow.

"That's what tiggers do best! Only tiggers don't climb trees, they bounce 'em!" Tigger exclaimed.

He headed straight for a tall tree and began to bounce up the branches.

Tigger and Roo bounced up,
up, up. Soon they were at the top
of the tree. Roo thought it was
great fun.

Tigger looked down. "How did this tree get so high?" he asked in a worried voice.

Then he began to shout "Hello-o-o!" He hoped that someone would hear and come help him.

Pooh and Piglet heard Tigger's cries.
"It's a jag-u-lar!" said Pooh. "They are one of
the fiercer animals."

But as they got closer, the pair realized it
was only Tigger and Roo.

"Hello!" Pooh called. "What are you doing
up there?"

"I'm all right, but
Tigger's stuck!" Roo
explained cheerfully.

Tigger was clinging to
the tree trunk for dear life.
"Get Christopher Robin!"
he begged. "He'll know
what to do!"

Soon Christopher Robin arrived with
Rabbit and Kanga. He instructed the others
to hold the sides of his coat to form a little
trampoline for Tigger and Roo to jump into.

Roo jumped first. "That was fun!" he squealed.

Then it was Tigger's turn. "Tiggers don't jump, they bounce!" he insisted. He was miserable. "If I ever get down from here, I promise never to bounce again," he said.

"I heard that, Tigger!" cried Rabbit.

Finally, Tigger
was convinced to
let go.

He sailed out of the
tree and landed safely
among his friends.

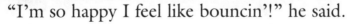

"I'm so happy I feel like bouncin'!" he said.

"But you promised!" Rabbit reminded him.

"You mean I can't bounce ever again?"
Tigger asked.

"Never!" Rabbit said, pleased to have finally
unbounced Tigger.

Tigger walked away, sad and droopy.

"I like the old bouncy Tigger best," Roo said.

"So do I," said Christopher Robin.

"We all do. Don't you agree, Rabbit?" asked Kanga.

"Oh, all right," Rabbit said reluctantly. "I suppose I like the old Tigger better, too."

Tigger came bouncing back. He was so
happy to have his bounces again that he got all
his friends to start bouncing too. Because, as
Tigger explained, "It makes you feel just grrreat!"

And even Rabbit had to admit he was right!